#3 Grasshopper Glitch

D0189127

Books in the S.W.I.T.C.H. series

S.W.I.T.C.H.

#3 Grasshopper Glitch

Ali Sparkes

illustrated by
Ross Collins

darbycreek

MINNEAPOLIS

Text © Ali Sparkes 2011
Illustrations © Ross Collins 2011

"SWITCH: Grasshopper Glitch" was originally published in English in 2011.
This edition is published by an arrangement with Oxford University Press.

Darby Creek
A division of Lerner Publishing Group, Inc.
241 First Avenue North
Minneapolis, MN 55401 U.S.A.

Website address: www.lernerbooks.com

Main body text set in ITC Goudy Sans Std. 14/19.
Typeface provided by Monotype Typography.

Library of Congress Cataloging-in-Publication Data

Sparkes, Ali.
      Grasshopper glitch / by Ali Sparkes ; illustrated by Ross Collins.
         p.   cm. — (S.W.I.T.C.H. ; #03)
      Summary: After accidentally drinking some of mad scientist Petty
Pott's SWITCH potion while at school, twins Josh and Danny become
grasshoppers and this time they may not change back without help.
      ISBN 978-0-7613-9201-9 (lib. bdg. : alk. paper)
      [1. Grasshoppers—Fiction. 2. Brothers—Fiction. 3. Twins—Fiction.
4. Science fiction.] I. Collins, Ross, ill. II. Title.
PZ7.S73712Gr 2013
[Fic]—dc23   2012026634

Manufactured in the United States of America
1 – SB – 12/31/12

For Elena

Danny and Josh
(and Piddle)

They may be twins, but they're NOT the same! Josh loves insects, spiders, beetles, and bugs. Danny can't stand them. Anything little with multiple legs freaks him out. So sharing a bedroom with Josh can be . . . erm . . . interesting. Mind you, they both love putting earwigs in big sister Jenny's underwear drawer . . .

Danny
- FULL NAME: Danny Phillips
- AGE: eight years
- HEIGHT: taller than Josh
- FAVORITE THING: skateboarding
- WORST THING: creepy-crawlies and cleaning
- AMBITION: to be a stuntman

Josh

- FULL NAME: Josh Phillips
- AGE: eight years
- HEIGHT: taller than Danny
- FAVORITE THING: collecting insects
- WORST THING: skateboarding
- AMBITION: to be an entomologist

Piddle

- FULL NAME: Piddle the dog Phillips
- AGE: two dog years (fourteen in human years)
- HEIGHT: not very
- FAVORITE THING: chasing sticks
- WORST THING: cats
- AMBITION: to bite a squirrel

Contents

Twitchy Travelers

Danny was jumpy.

"Stop making that *noise!*" snapped Josh as they waited at the gate. Danny was making a peculiar screechy-scrapey noise through his teeth. He was trying to learn to whistle. He only managed to sound like a rusty bike chain. A chain being repeatedly dragged against a tin tray.

He didn't pay Josh any attention.

"Will you *stop* it!" Josh whacked his lunch box against the back of Danny's head. His twin glared at him. He rubbed his spiky blond hair.

"I can't help it. I'm nervous!" Danny muttered, eyeing the car at the curb. The car that would take them to school this morning. Mom couldn't drive them in today. Their next-door neighbor, Petty Potts, was giving them a ride. She was just getting her bag from the house. Soon they would be going.

Josh stared at the car too. He felt that his brother had some cause to be jumpy. Petty's car was so old that it was actually made of *wood*. The back half of it looked like a chunk of old boat. The dark green leather seats inside were like furniture from a museum. Piddle, their terrier dog, was cocking his leg against one of the back wheels.

"It can't be legal to drive this around on regular roads!" hissed Danny. Petty emerged from her gate with a large open-topped woven straw bag in her hands. "I mean—do you think she's even got a license?"

"Come along, you two. Hop in," said Petty. She opened the door. She tipped forward the front passenger seat so they could get into the back.

"Oh, get away from my tires, you nasty leaky creature!" She glared at Piddle. He grinned up at her doggily. Then he shot back into the yard and up the side passage where they heard Mom shutting the gate.

Petty tutted and went around to the driver's door. She was in her brown raincoat. She was wearing her usual tweedy hat, pulled down low over her glasses. She looked exactly like someone should look driving such an ancient wreck, thought Danny. He made a face at Josh. They clambered in across the bouncy cracked leather seat. It also smelled like a museum.

"Where are the seat belts?" asked Josh looking left and right.

"It's a classic car, Josh," said Petty. She ground the gears as the engine coughed into life. "They didn't always put in seat belts back in 1966. Just hang on tight. I'm not going to crash." She turned around and put her bag in between them on the seat. She creased her face into what she probably thought was a reassuring smile.

Petty Potts's reassuring smiles never really worked somehow. Danny grabbed on to a little leather strap above the window. He narrowed his eyes at her.

Josh did the same.

"Oh, for heaven's sake, you two!" she huffed. She turned back and started to drive up the road in a lurching fashion. "You might have a little faith in me. I'm not going to kill you!"

Danny and Josh raised identical eyebrows at her in the rearview mirror. Petty had never *tried* to kill them, true. But she had certainly brought them closer to a bizarre and grisly death than any other grown-up they knew. They'd stumbled into a secret underground laboratory hidden beneath her garden shed. And they'd come close to being crushed, drowned, splatted, pecked hollow, swatted, mummified, and eaten. More times than they wanted to remember. Petty might *look* like a nice old biddy, but she was the genius inventor of SW.I.T.C.H. spray. It could change you into a creepy-crawly with just a few squirts. Josh and Danny had already been transformed into spiders and flies. And that was really quite enough.

Naming her *Serum Which Instigates Total Cellular Hijack* "S.W.I.T.C.H." made it sound rather fun. And it was. If you didn't mind getting eaten, drowned, turned into soup, or splattered with a giant sandal.

"Any more side effects from your housefly adventure?" Petty called back, cheerfully, over the rumble and clunk of the fifty-year-old engine.

"No. We've stopped sniffing around the trash can now," said Josh. "And Danny hasn't spat on a doughnut or tried to walk up the kitchen window since last Tuesday." He sighed and then grinned to himself. Being a bluebottle *was* very exciting. Even Danny had loved it. Well, apart from the bit when he'd been on the lunch menu for a hungry spider.

"Good, good, good," said Petty. "You know, I thought it was a disaster when you two first accidentally ran into a jet of my Spider S.W.I.T.C.H. spray. But actually it was the best thing that could have happened. If you hadn't found your way into my secret lab, I might never have moved on from trying to S.W.I.T.C.H. rats and dogs!"

"Er . . . thanks," muttered Josh, raising his eyebrows at Danny. He was shaking his head and looking annoyed. The dog Petty had been trying to spray was *their* dog, Piddle. It was when they were rescuing Piddle that they had first got caught in a jet of Petty's S.W.I.T.C.H. spray.

"And of course, rats could never tell me what the experience was like!" went on Petty. "And you two are so helpful! I'm so delighted you've agreed to be my assistants on the S.W.I.T.C.H. project."

"Look—we just said we'd help you out by looking for your missing cube things," said Josh. They reached the traffic lights near their school.

"We're *not* trying out any more S.W.I.T.C.H. sprays!"

"I never asked you to!" protested Petty. She looked all innocent and injured. "And finding my missing cubes is absolutely the most important thing. Without them I will never be able to rediscover my formula. Or be able to move on to turning things into reptiles. And you'll never get the chance to find out how it feels to be a giant python or an anaconda or a Komodo dragon!"

"We don't want to find out!" squawked Danny. "Haven't you heard us? Being turned into other creatures is just too dangerous!"

"Yes, of course, of course . . ." Petty smiled ferociously into her rearview mirror. "Although I can't imagine how anyone could hurt you if you were a twenty-four-foot python!"

Danny and Josh looked at each other. There was just the faintest twinkle of excitement in Josh's eyes. He thought about Petty's promise. If they could find the last four missing cubes that held the secret of the REPTOSWITCH spray, she would be able to temporarily turn them into amazing reptiles. Josh loved wildlife— being a lizard or a snake would be incredible! The BUGSWITCH was amazing enough but a REPTOSWITCH? It would be hard to resist trying *that* spray out. And nice to be less easy to eat or squash! This was a definite downside to being a creepy-crawly.

"Josh!" hissed Danny, narrowing his eyes at his brother. "Don't even *think* about it! You don't even know she's telling the truth! She's as fishy as fish fingers in fish sauce in a fish-shaped dish!"

Josh had to admit Danny was right. Petty claimed some pretty crazy things. She had the BUGSWITCH sprays figured out. But she insisted a man who had worked with her had stolen the rest of her research. She said he even burnt out bits of her memory. She'd forgotten where she'd hidden the special glass cubes that contained the secret REPTOSWITCH formula. That was why she needed their help to find them. And they *had* found one.

"We have been looking for your cubes," Danny was saying. "And we will keep looking for them. But don't think you'll ever change us into anything again. Not unless we agree to it!"

"Well, of course not! What do you take me for? Some kind of monster?" huffed Petty. "I would never dream of such a thing. But . . . I just wanted to tell you that I think I have perfected a S.W.I.T.C.H. potion now. You can *drink* S.W.I.T.C.H. instead of spray it on. It'll have the same effect."

"We're not drinking anything!" declared Josh.

"Of course you're not. But if you ever *did*, it's all quite safe. Look, there's a S.W.I.T.C.H. antidote potion too! I made it just in case drinking S.W.I.T.C.H. makes the changes last longer than the spray. It gets right inside, of course, so it probably lasts longer. But the antidote can stop it all at anytime like the gas back in my lab. I've got both the potion and the antidote in my bag." With one hand on the wheel, she turned around to rummage in the bag between them. She was just hauling out a small plastic bottle when Josh shouted,

"LOOK OUT!"

There was a screech of elderly brakes. All three of them jerked violently forward. Petty's car nearly collided with the crossing guard. School bags, lunch boxes, and Petty's stuff went flying everywhere. It was good that Josh and Danny had been hanging on to the little leather straps above their heads. They might well have shot through the windshield.

Petty had bashed her nose on her steering wheel. "Oh, all right! All right! Keep your stupid shiny hat on!" She was shouting at the crossing guard. He was waving his yellow STOP sign around and looking very angry.

"Please—just drive around the corner, so we can get out," wailed Josh. He kept his head down behind the front seats in case anyone from their school was watching. He and Danny scrabbled about, picking up their bags, books, and lunch boxes.

"My bun's all squashed!" moaned Danny. He picked up a sweet pastry bun that now looked more like a cookie.

"Well, mine had a pretty hard whack too. Thanks for your concern!" sniffed Petty. They pulled at last around the corner, away from the angry crossing guard.

"My buNNN! BuNNN—not BUM!" squawked Danny. He gave a horrified shudder.

"Thanks for the ride," said Josh. They fumbled with the tipping front seat and the passenger door. He and Danny grabbed their school stuff. They got out as fast as they could, slamming the door behind them.

Petty rubbed her nose. She called to them. "I'm off around the park to try the potion and the antidote out on the squirrels. I'll let you know how it goes!" She did a violent U-turn, nearly knocking a passing cyclist off his bike.

"Come on," said Danny. He shoved his drink and flattened pastry back into his lunch box. He slung his bag over his shoulder. "I never thought I'd say this, but I can't wait to get to school, where it's safe."

He went on through the school gates. He had no idea that something very, very *un*safe was slurping about in his bag.

Bad Soda

"Who *is* making that noise?" snapped Miss Mellor.

Everyone in the class froze and widened their eyes. Then they looked around for the culprit. The room was silent.

"That scrapey, scratchy noise! It's really irritating," went on Miss Mellor. She put down her spelling test grading, stood up, and folded her arms.

"Don't know, ma'am," muttered a few innocent pupils.

Josh nudged Danny, but his brother just shrugged.

"Well, whoever it was, stop it at once," commanded Miss Mellor. She sat down again, heavily. She picked up her red pen. She sent a warning glare around the classroom.

A few minutes passed as the class got on with "quiet reading." Then the noise began again. Scratch, scrape. Scratch, scrape. Scratch, scrape.

Josh nudged Danny again. But his brother was engrossed in his book. He was quite unaware that he was moving his legs up and down against each other. The seams of his new school pants and the Velcro tabs on his school shoes kept scraping and scratching.

"Teacher! It's him! It's Danny," called Claudia Petherwaite. She pointed at her classmate with a smug look on her face. Josh narrowed his eyes at her.

"Danny. What on earth are you doing?" demanded Miss Mellor. "You sound like some kind of insect!"

"Sorry, ma'am," mumbled Danny, looking a little pink. "I didn't know I was doing it."

"Well, now you *do*, stop it!" She sat down again and snatched up her pen once more. She was not in a good mood.

Claudia smirked at Danny, who stuck his tongue out at her. He managed to keep quiet for the rest of the lesson.

Just before lunch Miss Mellor stood up and did a sudden lunch box check. All that week the school had been working on a healthy eating project. Those who brought lunch from home had to show what was in their lunch boxes. They got a score out of ten for how healthy it was.

Those who had school lunch sat back and watched. *They* didn't have to go through this. But about fifteen kids went to get their lunch boxes to open them for inspection.

"Not bad, Billy," said Miss Mellor. She peered into Billy Sutter's plastic lunch box. "Egg and watercress. White bread though. Should be whole wheat really. Raisins . . . good . . ."

Josh and Danny peered anxiously into their lunch boxes. Their lunches were as identical as they were. Ham sandwiches, grapes, a sweet pastry bun, and a soda. The bread was white though.

"Claudia, what's in yours?" asked Miss Mellor. Claudia opened her little basket-weave box as if it were a birthday present.

"I've got homemade whole wheat rolls. They're filled with organic roasted vegetables and low-fat hummus," she declared proudly.

"Hummus? Isn't that something you get off the compost heap?" hissed Danny. Miss Mellor clucked approvingly at Claudia.

"And I have crudités," went on Claudia. She held aloft a little bundle of cut-up carrot and cucumber sticks. "With wild mushrooms and couscous."

"Couscous? Sounds like the cat bringing up fur balls," muttered Danny.

"Looks like it too," said Josh. Claudia held out something sludgy in a dainty plastic dish.

"And what do you have for dessert?" asked Miss Mellor.

"Oh, Mommy doesn't give me a dessert," said Claudia. She glowed with pride. "She says sugar rots my teeth. I do nibble on sun-dried mango. But only on weekends."

"Gosh." Even Miss Mellor looked slightly appalled. "And to drink . . . ?"

"Just water, of course. Soda is full of sugar. And the sugar-free stuff kills children's brain cells," explained Claudia. She closed her lunch box with a satisfied snap.

Miss Mellor moved on to Danny and Josh with a rather fixed grin. Then she peered down into their open lunch boxes. "Hmm . . . that looks OK. Some fruit. White bread, though—tsk! And pastries?"

"There are raisins in them!" said Josh hopefully. But Miss Mellor's lips didn't unpurse. She lifted Danny's plastic bottle out. "Soda?"

"Yep. Lemon," said Danny, with a sassy grin. "Full of sugar! Yeah!"

"Your teeth will drop out!" cooed Claudia, happily, as the bell for lunch rang.

"I'll risk it!" said Danny. Miss Mellor went back to her desk. He unscrewed the bottle and took

a slurp. "Ugggg!" he spluttered. "This isn't our usual soda! Yuck! Mom must have got some different stuff by mistake."

Josh put his schoolwork into his desk. He unwrapped his sandwiches. The "cold lunchers" ate at their desks while the "hot lunch" crowd went off to the lunchroom. "Better just get some water from the sink in the bathroom then," he said.

Danny didn't say anything.

Josh took a big bite of his sandwich. "Great ham, though," he mumbled. His mouth was full. "Ham's my favorite. What's yours?"

"Chirrup."

Josh looked around at the chair next to him. Danny's lunch box was open. His sandwiches half unwrapped. His bottle of yucky soda still had its lid off. Danny was nowhere to be seen. He must have gone for water.

But sitting on his blue plastic seat, chirruping was a bright green grasshopper. Josh grinned. That'd give Danny a scare when he got back.

It was only a matter of seconds before the screaming started. Daisy and Emily spotted the grasshopper first. It suddenly launched itself through the air and landed on their table.

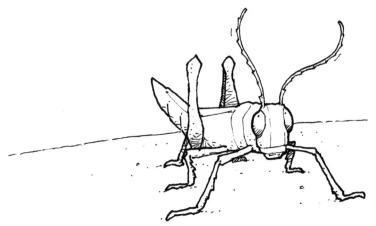

Claudia dropped her couscous and began to squeal. She backed away from the long-legged beast crouching on the nearby desk.

"What *is* going on?" demanded Miss Mellor.

"Eeeeeeww! It's a grasshopper! A grasshopper!" shrieked Daisy, Emily, and Claudia. Several other girls began to scream now. The grasshopper launched itself up into the air. It landed, half a second later, on Miss Mellor's desk. Craig Thomas, who was standing nearby, also gave a little shriek. He tried to turn it into a cough. Three or four other boys were looking very uneasy.

"Josh!" called Miss Mellor, looking rather edgy herself. "Can you catch it, please?" Everyone knew that Josh was crazy about creepy-crawlies. Danny called him "a freaky little bug geek."

Josh ran across to her desk and opened his hands. "Come on. Come on, little fella!" he coaxed. The grasshopper turned around and looked at him. It rubbed its impressive back legs together and chirruped again.

Josh wished that Danny was there to see it. It was a beautiful shiny green meadow grasshopper. It had a rather endearing way of tilting its shiny green head and waving its shiny green front legs.

Almost as if it was trying to say something to him!

"Danny, come and see this!" called out Josh glancing around the room. But there was still no sign of his brother. Danny might have freaked out anyway. He didn't like grasshoppers.

The grasshopper waved harder. It was doing a little dance now! Amazing! If Danny were here, he'd have stopped being scared by now. He would be laughing! He'd be waving back! He'd be . . .

Josh suddenly felt cold. His eyes bulged. He was replaying something in his mind. The near-crash in Petty Potts's car that morning. All the lunch box stuff and the bits and pieces in Petty's bag, flying around. Then he saw Petty talking to them. Telling them about the drinkable S.W.I.T.C.H. potion, which she was taking to the park.

Josh stared back at Danny's desk, at the open bottle. He could see that it was not the same bottle as his own. And their bottles, like the rest of their lunch, were normally identical.

OH NO! yelled a loud, panicky voice in his head. DANNY! DANNY DRANK S.W.I.T.C.H. POTION!

"Well, go on, Josh," said Miss Mellor. "Pick it up! I want it off my desk!" Four or five curious classmates had now clustered around Josh. The grasshopper was still waving at him. Rather frantically.

"Danny!" Josh whispered, holding out his palm. "Get on my hand!"

"Just pick it *up*, Josh," snapped his teacher. "Before it hops off somewhere else."

"Don't worry," said Billy Sutter, holding a heavy math book. "I'll get it."

And before Josh could start to scream "NOOOOO!" Billy slammed the book down.

Toilet Trouble

"DANNEEEEE!" shrieked Josh, horrified. His classmates had crowded around. They were ghoulishly waiting to see the mashed insect. They wondered why Josh was shrieking for his brother.

With a trembling hand, Josh reached out and lifted the heavy book. He gulped hard. Tears blurred his vision as he steeled himself to witness Danny squished flat all over Miss Mellor's ink-stained desk.

The book lifted and the rest of the class held its breath. Underneath was . . .

"Nothing! It must have hopped off!" grumbled Billy, disappointed.

"There it is! On Josh's hair!" squealed Daisy. Billy picked up the book, ready to thwack it down on Josh's head. The grasshopper was too

fast though. It shot across the room onto the
bookshelf. Then to the top of the paint cupboard.
More screaming erupted. Then it landed on the
windowsill. Billy ran toward it, the heavy book
raised up in one fist. The grasshopper shot out
through the open window.

"Phew! Drama over," said Miss Mellor.

Josh stared out of the window, horror-struck. Miss Mellor turned to write on the whiteboard. Then he ran back to Danny's desk, grabbed the bottle, and screwed its lid on tight. He ran back across the classroom. He jumped up onto the low windowsill. Outside, a sidewalk led past the window. On the other side of it, the school field stretched away toward some trees and bushes.

Danny could be anywhere! Josh looked behind him. The remaining kids in the class were getting on with their lunch now. Miss Mellor still had her back to him. Josh didn't wait any longer. He jumped out of the window, landing on the sidewalk. Then he ran out onto the field.

"Danny!" he shouted, desperately staring around the grass and bushes. "Danny! Where are you?"

He listened hard. All he could hear were the shrieks of kids on the playground on the other side of the school.

Even if Danny was chirruping at the top of his voice, there was no way Josh would hear him. Josh sank to his knees and put his face right into the

grass. "DAANNNEEEEE!" he wailed into it. He knew
it was hopeless. His brother could be anywhere.
Worse, he might already be inside a blackbird.

Then something pinged against his ear. He lifted
his head. Danny dropped
onto his open palm.
At least, he thought it
was Danny. It could be
another grasshopper.

"Danny?" murmured Josh, waving a finger at the
insect. It waved its short feelers back. "It is you.
Isn't it?!" The grasshopper waved again. "OK. If
that's you, waggle your left feeler!" The insect
did. Josh heaved a huge sigh of relief. He nearly
blew Danny back into the grass.

"What are we going to do? You drank S.W.I.T.C.H.
potion! And we've got math in half an hour. How
am I going to explain this to Miss Mellor?"

Danny offered a number of suggestions.
He scraped his back legs and wings together
frantically, creating that chirruping noise. It was
clear that he had quite a lot to say. But Josh
couldn't understand a word of it. He stared
anxiously around the field. He clutched the potion
bottle in one hand. He wondered what on earth
to do. If only one of them had also picked up the
antidote! He knew he hadn't. He'd drunk some of
his soda. It was the usual stuff.

"Wait, though. Petty took the antidote with her
to the park," he said. "Maybe she's still there! It's
not far away. Yes! That's the answer. We have
to get to Petty. I think I can make it there in five
minutes if I run."

Josh stood up, Danny cupped in his hand. He
ran toward the school gate that led out to the
street. The park was only a short walk away. Petty
might be there still, wondering why the lemon
soda wasn't working on the squirrels.

Desperately, he hoped no teacher or lunch
lady would notice him. Josh ran along the side
of the school where the boys' bathrooms were.

He reached the corner of the building. Then Billy Sutter and his friend Jason Bilk stepped out of the outside bathroom door. They bumped into him.

"Hey! Watch where you're going!" grunted Jason. Billy noticed immediately that Josh had something in his hand.

"What's that?" he asked. He prodded a muddy finger at Josh's closed hand. A chirrup came from inside it. "You got that grasshopper again? You made it a pet or something?" Billy and Jason pried open Josh's hand, despite his squawks of protest. Danny looked up, waggling his feelers anxiously.

"I'm gonna get it this time!" chuckled Billy. He slapped his hand down. But Danny had shot away like a green rubber band before he could be squashed. Now he was on the floor by the open bathroom door. At once Jason and Billy started trying to stamp on him.

"NO! LEAVE HIM ALONE!" shrieked Josh. He chased them into the bathroom where Danny had jumped next. Billy and Jason were clomping about wildly all over the damp concrete floor. They shouted "Get it! Get it!" Josh stood, aghast, feeling totally helpless. Then there was a flicker of movement. He spotted his brother in a stall. Josh threw himself inside it, slamming the door behind him. He firmly locked it as Danny leapt onto the toilet paper holder, looking very agitated.

"Are you OK?" hissed Josh just as there was a break in the stamping. Both boys outside heard him clearly. They let out peals of laughter.

"Oh, wittle Hoppy Woppy! Are you hurt?" said Jason, in a drippy voice. Billy squealed with mirth.

"Come on—come out! Bring out your little pet!" chortled Jason. "We'll only stamp on him once."

Josh hoped if he just said nothing, they might get bored and go away. Five minutes later, they were still banging on the stall door and jeering. If they kept this up much longer, there would be no time to get to the park and find Petty before he and Danny were supposed to be back in class. They'd be in big trouble. He could just wait here, hoping that Danny would switch back again. But he had no idea how long it might take. Petty hadn't known either. That's why she'd made the antidote. And if Danny did suddenly switch back, how would they explain it to the two boys outside the stall? The high narrow window above him was way too small for anyone to crawl in or out of.

"Hey—GIVE ME A LEG UP!" said Billy.

Josh groaned.

There had to be some way out of this. Then he blinked. He stared at the bottle in his hand. There it was. The only escape. He put Danny up on the ledge by the window, which was slightly open.

Two rows of fingers hooked over the top of the stall door with a thud. Josh unscrewed the bottle's lid and drank two gulps.

The grunts and scuffles on the other side got louder. He put the lid back on and hid the bottle behind the toilet.

Seconds later, Billy, puffing with effort, peered down into the stall with confusion.

Josh had vanished.

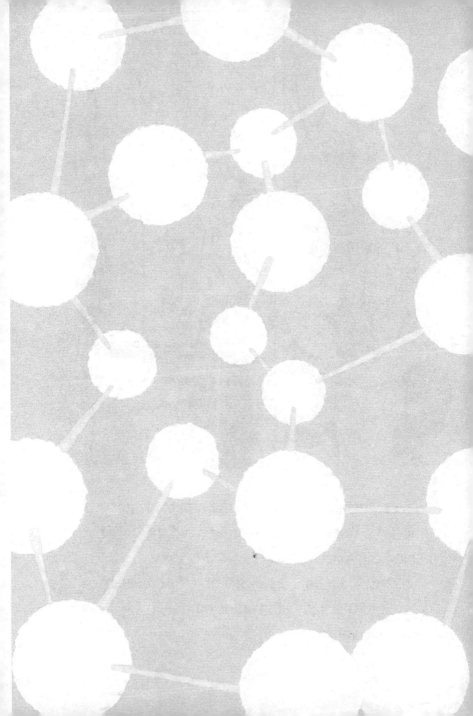

A Whisker from Death

"WHEEEEEEEEEEEEEEEEEE!" yelled Josh as he flung himself through the air. His back legs were like a huge slingshot. They shot him high above the forest of grass below him. Only the slingshot came along for the ride too.

"It's great, isn't it?" called back Danny. He had had twelve minutes more practice at being a grasshopper than his brother. "As soon as I switched, I just had to jump! Even though I was scared. I just had to! We can fly too! See—we're flying!" The stiff little wings on his back opened out like a short green cape. They helped him to glide on and on through the warm air. They were already out of the school. They'd jumped down from the bathroom window, across the field, and over the high hedge without any problem at all.

"This is the best creepy-crawly we've been yet!" laughed Josh. He opened his own wings and glided along behind Danny. Far below him flashed a green garden and a blur of blue-white pond. Insects the size of dogs flew past them. Some were making noises like small jets. Others were more like helicopters.

THWUMP! THWUMP! They landed side by side on a gray brick wall. They turned to inspect each other's shiny new grasshopper bodies. They each had two sets of fairly normal-sized insect legs. They were surprisingly muscular with little hooky feet—or hands. But their hind legs were three times bigger and bent back behind them in a upside-down *V*. Their eyes were large and round with short feelers set above them like pointy eyebrows. Josh thought Danny's long face looked rather solemn. Then his brother started wiggling his little fingerlike mouthparts about with enthusiasm.

"What are Billy and Jason going to think when they find you've disappeared?" he giggled. His voice was not too unlike his own considering he had a grasshopper's mouth.

"I'm more worried about what Miss Mellor will think. We could get detention for a week!" said Josh. He rubbed his legs nervously against his wings.

"Ooh!" Making the noise himself, it was incredibly loud and croaky. "That's how grasshoppers make their chirruping noise!"

"Careful," said Danny, looking around. "It's bad enough being chased by stupid kids who want to squash you. You don't want to attract predators too! What eats grasshoppers, Josh?"

Josh gulped. "Well . . . we don't taste great. That's why we're quite bright green and shiny. It's to warn anything that wants to eat us that we're a bit—I dunno—sour. We're still not safe though. Birds, mice, snakes, spiders. All the usual ones. They'll try. We should keep moving. We need to get the antidote."

Danny nodded. "Which way, do you think?"

"That way," said Josh. He waved his feelers firmly to his left. He didn't know how he could be so sure. It was something to do with the way the sun was shining and the smell in the air. He felt a rumble inside him. He hadn't had much lunch.

"I'm starving," said Danny. They catapulted themselves high into the air again. Of course, he hadn't had any lunch at all. "Wooooo-hooo! Oh yeah! No, I'm really hungry."

"Of course," called Josh. He flew alongside his brother with his rather dashing green cloak wings.

"Grasshoppers are big eaters. They eat at least sixteen times their own body weight—every day! I'm hungry too. But we can't stop."

Three seconds later they stopped. They landed on a large leafy bush that grew up against a low brick wall. It smelled as good to them as a doughnut factory at snack time. Josh found himself cramming his mouth with thick, juicy chunks of green leaf.

Danny settled on a leaf next to him. He began to demolish it with loud chomping noises.

"Ooooooh, this is so good!" munched Danny. "How come we never ate leaves before? There's tons in our garden! We just ignore them . . ."

When the empty feeling inside him began to ease off, Josh looked up. He was surprised to see that Danny had stopped eating. Danny's big green eyes were bulging. Suddenly Danny spat out something brown and sticky right onto his lovely leaf.

"UGGGH! MANNERS, PLEASE!" said Josh. "Did you eat a gross piece?"

Danny shook his head. He stared at Josh, his enormous eyes shining like glass beads. Somewhere in his brain Josh knew that spitting brown stuff was a bad sign. It was something grasshoppers did when—

"JUMP!" yelled Danny. He pinged up into the sky. Which helped Josh to remember. Ah yes . . . grasshoppers chucked up brown goo out of fear. Usually fear of . . . PREDATORS!

All Josh saw, when he finally turned around, was a huge mouth. A gigantic pink diamond-shaped pair of jaws with sharp white fangs and a pointed pink tongue with hundreds of spikes on it. Blecch! He spat out his own brown blob.

His slingshot legs threw him high into the air.

But then he collided, with a whump, against a thick furry log, which was falling from the sky.

When five razor-sharp white claws shot out of it, Josh realized that it was actually a paw.

He found himself splatted back down on the leafy wall, with a gigantic furry face pressed right against him. A moist pink nose nudged him, and a fan of fine white spiky things drooped down on either side of him. Whiskers. A gust of meaty breath blew him over.

Josh realized he was about to be eaten by a cat.

In Ear

High above Josh, Danny clung to a springy twig. He stared down in horror at the enormous furry monster that was sniffing and biffing at his brother.

"JOOOOOOOOOOSH!" he bellowed. He couldn't hear anything except a scarily loud thrumming, wheezing noise. He realized it was the cat. The cat was purring! Poor Josh. He liked cats. So did Danny. Usually cats purred when they were getting some milk or being stroked. Not when they were about to bite you in half.

Danny jumped down onto the cat's head. He landed up to his armpits (or leg pits, depending on how you looked at it) in thick tabby fur. The cat's right ear flicked once. But it was so fascinated by its prey it didn't try to shake Danny off. Hanging on to the fur, Danny leaned out to see if Josh was OK.

At least he couldn't feel, hear, or—worse—smell the cat chewing on anything.

Far below he could see Josh trying to crawl away from the cat's paw, so he could jump away. But the cat kept following him along the top of the wall, keeping its paws or nose just above him, so he couldn't escape.

"JOSH!" yelled Danny, tilting his head back so he could hear better (his ears, it turned out, were on his belly). "Are you all right?"

"Yes—but I can't jump away. It's playing cat and mouse with me!" shouted back Josh.

"Maybe it won't eat you," called Danny, trying not to squeak with fright. "Maybe it just wants to play."

"Oh yes—that'll be it," squawked Josh, dodging a claw as it swiped past his feelers. "It only wants to be friends! In a "slash my head off" kind of way. That's nice then."

Danny racked his brain, trying to figure out what he could do. How could he distract the cat? He edged over its brow and wondered about jumping into its eye. But a thicket of eyebrow hairs, almost as long as its whiskers, sprouted out above the nearest glinting green orb. He'd never get past that before he got a claw stuck through his innards.

What about the ear though?

He hopped across to a triangular tent of cat skin and peered around the edge of it. It was a bit like a teepee inside, with tufts of fine fur lightly covering soft pink and gray skin. It was quite cozy, really. It was waggling about a bit as the cat's head switched from side to side, eagerly watching the tormented victim between its paws. There was even a pet in the ear tent. A surprised-looking flea was drinking what looked like juice through a straw poked somewhere down inside the tufty fur. The flea stared at Danny and paused, mid-slurp. There was a small pop and the straw snapped back into its brown shiny face. It burped. "Pardon!" it said. It waved a short, hairy, black foreleg in front of its mouthparts.

"Better out than in," said Danny.

"EEEAAARGH!" shrieked Josh below. The cat's mouth was descending on him again. Its spiky pale pink tongue was scooping out to flip him back between its razor-sharp teeth. He could see the roof of its mouth, a dome of tough, wet, ribbed skin. He knew he would be mashed against it any second now.

Danny lost no time. He jumped into the cat's ear and started rubbing his legs and wings together in a frenzy. The noise, in the confined space, was deafening. The flea hopped out in an instant.

"MEEEEEEEEEEEEEAAAAAAAAAAH!" yowled the cat. It flipped over like a furry tiddlywink, pounding both paws against its ear. Danny shot clear with just a millisecond to spare. Josh flipped up past him, looking very . . . well . . . green.

"Th-that . . . was t-too . . . c-close," he stuttered as they flew away. "I was just about to be cat chewing gum."

They both shuddered with relief as they flew down over the fence around the park.

"We've got to get to Petty. We can't risk any more stops," said Josh. He looked left and right as they glided low across the grass. "It's not safe down there!"

VROOOOOM! Danny ducked in the air. He swooped sideways as a dark shadow flitted past him. "It's not safe up here, either!" he yelled. He looked up to see a dark flash of feathers and claws zooming around in a circle above them. A starling. Its sleek oil-colored feathers glinted in the sun. It turned back to have another try at pecking him out of the air.

"DOWN!" shrieked Josh. He dropped like a stone into the grass. Danny followed. Two thuds later, they were hidden in a thicket of green that rose just above their heads. Breathlessly they

crouched and waited. "Don't move!" whispered Josh. "It will only see us if we move." The starling swooped low over the grass. It made an ear-splitting screechy noise and then flew away.

"It didn't see us!" gasped Danny. "It couldn't make us out. Look! We're exactly the same color as the grass!"

"Camouflage," said Josh. His feelers quivered with shock. "We're meadow grasshoppers. Designed to look nearly invisible in grass."

"OK, so we're quite safe here then," sighed Danny. "But how are we ever going to find Petty Potts if we can't leap up and look around? And what time is it? We'll be late back to school, and then we'll be in trouble. Oh—this is so not good! I thought we might get to have a bit of fun for a change. But oh no, we're just fast food with feelers, as usual." He spat out another blob of brown goo. "Sorry."

Sit Tight

Petty Potts was annoyed. She'd managed to entice three or four squirrels over to her bench in the last hour. Each of them had scampered off with her special peanuts.

She knew, obviously, that there wasn't much point in trying to get a squirrel to swig a bit of strange-looking potion out of a plastic bottle. No, she had brought a tin cup along in her bag. She'd put a little of the potion into it. Then she dropped some peanuts in it and made them good and S.W.I.T.C.H.y. Then she set the peanuts down, one by one, at the far end of the wooden park bench. She waited for the bold squirrels to show up and steal them. She had been careful to wear disposable plastic gloves. She had no intention of S.W.I.T.C.H.ing herself!

One day she might, but she was quite old and might not recover from it.

Petty dug deep into her coat pocket. She pulled out a little green velvet box. Opening it up, she gazed wistfully at the two shining glass cubes inside it. She picked up one of them. She held it up to the light. It sparkled in the sun. The hologram of a tiny lizard could be clearly seen inside it.

"One out of six!" she sighed. She put the cube back in the box, next to the other cube. It had a slightly different hologram inside it. She sighed. "Two out of six. Which adds up to one-third of the formula to make REPTOSWITCH. Well, I'm glad to have you two," she murmured at the cubes. "But what about the other four, eh? Where did I hide the others? If only that scurrilous waste of space Victor Crouch hadn't burnt out my memory, I would know! I'd have the bug formula and the reptile formula. There might even be mammal or bird formula one day, for all I know! But if Josh and Danny don't find the rest of your little cube family, I may never know!"

Nobody was nearby to hear Petty talking to herself. That was probably just as well. Petty talked to herself quite a lot. She found it was the only way to get an intelligent answer.

"Of course, they don't understand how important this is. I am changing the world! But all they're worried about is getting to school on time. Honestly! Children today have no sense of adventure."

Petty snapped the little green box shut and put it on her lap. She trained her binoculars back onto the little family of four squirrels. They were running around a warm patch of grass beneath the oak trees. Still no change. Obviously the potion wasn't working as well as the spray. Those squirrels should be hopping about looking very green and confused by now. They should be getting panicky about their sudden lack of bushy tails.

If only she could see just one grasshopper! "AARRGH!" Suddenly a huge grasshopper loomed in front of her. It took a second or two of frantic flapping around her head before Petty realized she was still looking through the binoculars. The grasshopper was right on the lens.

"You crazy old baggage!" she scolded herself. She turned the binoculars around to peer at the insect on the lens. Maybe the potion had worked after all! But . . . no . . . all four squirrels were still racing around the grass.

"Just a regular grasshopper," she muttered. She flicked it away. It landed with a small click, by her

left shoe. Then it started to disco dance. Another grasshopper hopped along and joined it. They shimmied left and then right. They whirled their feelers in the air as if they were auditioning for *High School Musical.*

Unfortunately, Petty wasn't looking. She was examining the S.W.I.T.C.H. potion bottle more closely. Suddenly she slapped her palm against her forehead. "You lunatic!" she said, crossly, to herself. "You pudding-brained clod! This is the antidote! Not the potion." Now she began to rummage in her bag. "Where did I put the potion? And why did I use two of the same kind of bottle? Tsk! Oh, how annoying! The potion bottle must have fallen out in the car."

"It's not working," said Josh. He gave up on the disco dance routine. "She's not looking. We'll have to jump up on her knee. If we don't get that antidote soon we might never get back to school—or home—again!"

"Won't we just change back again anyway, after it's worn off?" said Danny. "We did last time."

"I don't know," said Josh. "This is the potion version, remember, not the spray. We've never drunk it before. It might last forever for all we know! But if we stay out here much longer, we'll just get eaten anyway. Oh will you stop that?"

"Sorry," said Danny. He kicked away another brown blob of panic goo.

"Come on—onto her knee!" said Josh. He was just about to jump when a shadow fell across them. He looked up and saw the vast bulk of another human. "Oh no! Someone's come and sat on the bench with her! We can't change back in front of someone else. Even if we do get to the antidote!"

"Morning, Miss Potts," shouted Mr. Grant. He lived around the corner.

Petty sighed. "Hello, Mr. Grant." The last thing she needed was some nosy neighbor interfering in her experiment. She put the bottle back into her bag.

"We have to get Petty to notice us!" insisted Danny. He glanced around nervously and gulped. "I don't care who sees! I'm not staying here to get eaten."

"Nice place to sit and watch the world go by, isn't it?" yelled Mr. Grant. He was a bit deaf. He didn't seem to realize that not everybody else was too.

"Hmm," said Petty. She tried not to wrinkle her nose. Mr. Grant smelled of stale coffee and unwashed socks. He had liked her for years.

"What's this then?" shouted Mr. Grant. He suddenly picked the little green box up from the bench where it had slid from Petty's lap. He flipped it open without even asking. He peered at the two glass cubes. "Oh! Very pretty!" he grinned, showing off his dark yellow teeth.

"Do you mind?" Petty wrestled the box from him. She jammed it deep down into her coat pocket.

"I've got one of those on my mantelpiece," belted out Mr. Grant.

"I very much doubt it," said Petty, crisply.

"Found it in a bird's nest!" he bawled on. "A year ago, when I was cutting down my old hedge. Some magpie had got it. Gave it a wash and put it next to my clock, I did."

Petty stared at him, her mouth open.

"Nice to find someone to share a bench with," Mr. Grant shouted, romantically. "Especially at this time of day! When there are no screaming kids about. They should keep 'em all in school a bit longer, I say. Getting out at three? Nonsense. Lock 'em up with their teachers until six o'clock. Give us oldies a chance to have a park bench to ourselves, eh? Ha-ha-ha!"

Petty was still trying to figure out whether she had really heard Mr. Grant say he had a S.W.I.T.C.H. cube on his mantelpiece. Then two grasshoppers jumped up onto her knee and began to wave. Petty blinked. Then her eyes stretched wide, but she didn't say anything.

"Don't you think?" barked Mr. Grant.

"Oh no," said Petty. She stared at her knee. She suddenly realized where the missing S.W.I.T.C.H. potion must have ended up. "It's Josh and Danny!"

"Don't you?" screamed Mr. Grant. "Don't you think it's nice here? No annoying kids. Just you and me! Ha-ha-ha!" And he slapped his hand down on her knee.

Petty shrieked.

"Oh come on!" roared Mr. Grant. "I'm only being friendly!"

But Petty was staring in horror at her knee. Only seconds before, Josh and Danny had been waving at her there. That idiot Grant had surely just splatted them across her skirt.

She smacked his hand away. She gasped with relief. There was no sign of splatted insect. A chirruping noise made her look down at the little tin cup on the bit of bench between her and her nasty neighbor. Inside the cup there was still a puddle of antidote (which she had mistaken for potion). It was leftover from the peanut dunking. Two grasshoppers were wallowing about in it.

"No need to be hoity-toity!" Mr. Grant was shouting. "I was only saying how nice it was to be here all on our own. Without any irritating, snotty-nosed schoolkids taking up all the benches and—DOOF!" Mr. Grant was abruptly shoved sideways as two schoolkids appeared out of thin air on the bench between him and Petty Potts.

Petty hooted with laughter. Mr. Grant fainted. By the time he'd regained his senses, he was alone. He took himself off to see the doctor.

"Sorry the boys are late," smiled Petty. She put her head around the classroom door. Josh and Danny sidled back to their desks. "I had a bit of an emergency. They were helping me."

"Oh," said Miss Mellor, checking her watch. "Well, it's only ten minutes. I suppose I don't have to mark it down. What kind of emergency?"

"They had to save me from something creepy-crawly! You know how good Josh is with that kind of thing," said Petty. She did her best "nice old dear" face. She pushed the S.W.I.T.C.H. potion bottle deep into her straw bag. Josh had run into the bathroom to get it for her just before they came back into class.

"See you at dismissal, boys," said Petty. She hurried out of the classroom.

"You didn't eat lunch, either of you!" scolded Miss Mellor. "Your lunch boxes are still out on your desks!"

"It's OK, Miss Mellor," Danny grinned. "We had a lot of salad stuff while we were out. Couldn't eat another thing!"

"Really? Sounds very healthy," said Miss Mellor, looking suspicious.

"It was!" said Josh. "And we're going to eat more leaves when we get home. Even more than Claudia! We're going to snarf a whole hedge. It tastes great!"

Bug-Eyed Burglary

"You must be joking!" Danny held up his hands and shook his head. "No way!"

"But you promised you'd help me!" insisted Petty. "You said you would help me get back all my REPTOSWITCH cubes! Remember—you said you wanted to try out being a python one day. Or a lizard—or an alligator!"

"We didn't say that! You did!" argued Josh.

"Oh nonsense!" Petty slammed the green velvet box down on her kitchen table. She had lured Josh and Danny in, as they arrived home from school. She used the pretense that she was worried about them after yesterday's grasshopper adventure. "I know you want to be an alligator, Josh! You're an eight-year-old boy, for heaven's sake. There would be something seriously wrong with you if you didn't!"

Josh looked at Danny. Petty was right. He did want to try out the REPTOSWITCH one day. Who wouldn't? Danny bit his lip. Josh knew his twin wanted to try it too.

Petty flicked open the box. She pointed to the four empty dents where the missing S.W.I.T.C.H. cubes belonged. She fixed them with a fanatical stare. "One more of these will mean we are

halfway there! Halfway toward being able to switch humans into reptiles! Imagine what we could do with that! It's fantastic enough being able to switch you into insects and spiders. But imagine what you could do in reptile form!"

"OK—we said we'd help you look," said Josh. "And we have been helping. We've been all over your garden and our yard. And we always check out anything we see in the street that shines a bit like glass. But this is different. You're asking us to be burglars!"

"Oh, pee, pickle, and poo!" snorted Petty. "I'm just asking you to take one teensy-weensy sip of potion. Just pop back to being a grasshopper and jump through Mr. Grant's mailbox. Then collect my S.W.I.T.C.H. cube from his mantelpiece and come out with it. No harm done. He won't even notice."

Josh and Danny looked at each other. There was only the slightest hint on their faces that maybe they might possibly think about Petty's plan. She spotted it and immediately held up a tiny glass dropper. It was already filled with S.W.I.T.C.H.

potion. "I've measured it out exactly for your height and weight and body mass," she said. "It will last precisely ten minutes. Long enough for me to get you to the house. Then five minutes to get inside to find the cube and change back to your human form. Then get the cube back to me. Mr. Grant's out. Wednesday afternoon he always goes to the casino."

Josh and Danny looked at each other again. Danny shrugged. "Sounds simple enough."

"EXCELLENT!" said Petty, holding up the dropper. "TONGUES OUT!"

Petty hid the grasshoppers in her coat pocket. They were safely tucked into a small plastic tub with holes in the lid so there was plenty of air to breathe. It was not a pleasant journey. They were jogging along in the tub, which smelled of old curry.

"I hope she's right about this S.W.I.T.C.H. cube being in Mr. Grant's house," muttered Danny. "We could be at home now, playing with Piddle or filling up the wading pool. Not stuck in a plastic tub in a crazy old scientist's pocket,

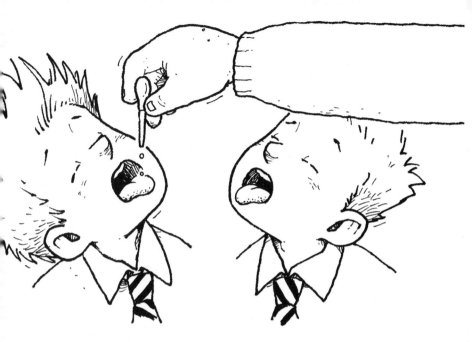

trying not to be sick. I'm only just holding back the panic goo here, you know!" His green face went a little greener.

Petty had told their mom her sons were helping out in the garden for half an hour. Mom thought that was a nice thing for Josh and Danny to do. She believed Petty was a lovely, harmless old lady.

Suddenly there was a flash of light as the tub rose out of the darkness of Petty's coat pocket. The lid abruptly snapped off and a fresh breeze

blew in. Josh and Danny clambered warily up to
the rim of the tub. They saw that it was being
held up against a long blue cliff, with a rectangle
cave set into it. "It's his mailbox, in his door," said
Josh. "She's putting us through!"

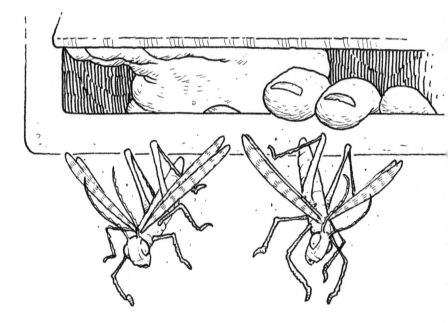

Sure enough, the dull yellow metal at the
back of the "cave" suddenly flapped backward.
Petty's enormous pink fingers poked at it. Josh
and Danny leapt through the gap and found

themselves gliding down through the cool indoor air of the hallway. They landed on the rough bristles of a doormat, next to a gigantic folded newspaper.

"BURGLARY ON THE INCREASE" read the front-page headline. It made Josh and Danny feel guilty.

"Come on—we haven't got much time," said Josh. He sprang down the hallway and into the living room. He bounded up onto the mantelpiece above the fireplace in one easy leap. The long pine shelf was full of clutter. Pictures, ornaments, matchboxes, tobacco tins, a pair of pliers, a jar of screws, and lots of thick fluffy dust.

"Eeeww!" whimpered Danny. He was frozen on the other side of the jar of screws, his green mouthparts twitching with disgust. At his feet lay a large, upside-down spider. Hairy, crispy, the color of straw. It was bigger than Danny. It was a good thing it was dead.

"Just turn around and hop away!" advised Josh. He couldn't believe, after all Danny had been

through, that he was still scared of a dead spider. Although, he supposed, Danny *had* been the one who was very nearly eaten by a spider a little while back.

Danny turned around and hopped away. Then he let out a chirrup of excitement. "It's here! I've found it!"

Josh jumped along the mantelpiece. He found his brother staring at a large, clear, perfectly cut cube of glass. Even through a layer of dust, it sparkled with rainbow light. Inside, delicately carved by laser, was the hologram of a snake. Its diamond-patterned body was coiled like rope and its head raised up, as if ready to strike. "It's beautiful," murmured Danny. He wondered which part was the one-sixth of Petty's secret formula.

"It is," agreed Josh. "Uh-oh!" He felt a strange tingling and knew what was coming. "Better get off the mantel—OW!" He sat up on the carpet. He rubbed his head where it had smacked against the brick fireplace. "That was a quick change!" He hadn't even had a second to hop down off the mantelpiece before he'd thwacked back into being a boy.

A moment later, Danny fell on his face.

"MMM-OW!" Josh shoved Danny off. "You could've aimed somewhere else!"

"Sorry," said Danny, as he picked himself up. "Didn't have time."

He turned and quickly collected the S.W.I.T.C.H. cube from the mantelpiece. He shoved it deep into his school pants pocket.

"WHAT ON EARTH IS ALL THIS?" yelled a voice from the hallway.

Josh and Danny froze, horrified. They were in the middle of burgling Mr. Grant's house—and he was IN IT!

Cubes, Cackling, and Cake

Mr. Grant appeared in the doorway, looking furious—at the newspaper in his hand. He was staring at the headline and shaking his head.

"What's all this?" he thundered. "Burglaries on the increase? Stuff and nonsense." He flipped over the paper as two small burglars slid down behind his old leather armchair. "Tennis club faces closure!" he bellowed. "Rubbish! All newspapers are rubbish!"

Then he stomped across the room. He thumped down into the armchair, sending up a cloud of dust around it. Josh and Danny, squashed behind it, held their breath and scrunched up their eyes. Josh felt a sneeze build up in his nose. He pinched the end of it, desperately. If he sneezed, they would be found out.

"Whoo-hoo!" called a voice and the doorbell clanged. Mr. Grant, being rather deaf, had fitted an extra-loud bell. "Whoo-hoo!" called the voice again. It was Petty Potts, trying to sound sweet.

"What?" yelled Mr. Grant and hurried out to the door.

"She's distracting him so we can get out!" hissed Danny. He was right. As soon as the door was opened, Petty invited herself right in. She began to propel Mr. Grant down the hallway, past the living room, and on into the kitchen.

"I was wondering if you could lend me some TEA!" she was shouting. "I've run out and I have friends coming. No time to run to the store!" It was a pretty feeble excuse, but it was good enough for Josh and Danny. They sprang out from behind the armchair and dashed out through the hallway. Seconds later, they were out on the pavement, hiding behind the front hedge.

"Thank you so much!" trilled Petty. She backed away down Mr. Grant's driveway. "And really sorry about your funny turn in the park yesterday. I do hope it doesn't happen again. Real children are bad enough without imaginary ones popping up on park benches!"

"Thanks!" mumbled Danny as all three of them ran down the street.

"Did you get it? Did you get it?" hissed Petty.

"Yes! Yes!" hissed back Danny.

"You might say thank you!" said Josh.

"Look, you're not the only ones who had to make a sacrifice!" huffed Petty. "I had to agree to go on a date with Old Yellow Teeth, back there, to give you two enough time to escape!"

In Petty's kitchen, Danny took out the S.W.I.T.C.H. cube and put it on the table.

"Oh, how wonderful!" sighed Petty. She scooped it up and turned it over in her palm. "Three out of six! We are halfway there!" She opened the green box and pressed the new cube in beside the other two. "One day soon," she murmured, standing straight and letting out a crazy cackle, "we will have them ALL! And then there will be NO STOPPING ME! Then I'll get you back, VICTOR CROUCH! I'LL GET YOU. I don't know how yet—but I'LL GET YOU!"

She was still shaking her fist, cackling, and staring into the middle distance when she finally noticed Josh and Danny folding their arms and giving her a look.

"Any chance you can stop doing the evil genius thing now and give us a bit of cake?" asked Danny.

"Oh, all right then," said Petty.

Top Secret!

For Petty Potts's Eyes Only!!

SUBJECT: REPTOSWITCH CUBE RETRIEVAL

Excellent news! Working with Josh and Danny really paid off today. I persuaded them to S.W.I.T.C.H. into grasshoppers again and get into Yellow Teeth Grant's house to get back my third REPTOSWITCH cube.

Of course, the jig was nearly up when the smelly duffer turned out to be at home when he was meant to be out. But I managed to use the old Potts charm to distract him while the boys ran outside (note to self: have still got it!).

And also very useful to know that my calculations on how long the grasshopper spray would last were right on!

REMEMBER

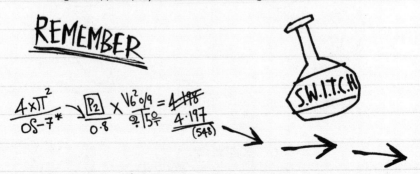

$$\frac{4 \times \pi^2}{OS-7^*} \searrow \frac{\boxed{P_2}}{0.8} \times \frac{\sqrt{6}^2 \, 0/9}{9 \sqrt{5^\circ}_T} = \frac{4.148}{4.197} \underset{(548)}{}$$

Amazed that I persuaded the boys to S.W.I.T.C.H. again after their experiences yesterday. They nearly got stamped on and eaten by a cat this time. It would be rather unfortunate if they got squashed or digested before we get much further. I'm quite fond of them in a way, but imagine the blow to science!

Still, the idea of being a giant reptile one day seems to be keeping them engaged. And speaking of giant reptiles, I am going to find out where Victor Crouch is working now. Maybe he is still in the secret government laboratories under Berkshire. Maybe I will be able to get back in. I bet he's still got that weird spiky, black fingernail. I wonder if he's grown any eyebrows back yet after that body hair experiment went wrong. I hope not. A man like Victor Crouch doesn't deserve a decent set of eyebrows. One day, I am going to find him, confront him, and make him confess that he stole my work and burnt out my memory.

But in the meantime, as far as Josh and Danny are concerned, I will keep my promise and will never make them try any more spray or potion. Or trick them. Or bribe them. OR anything like that. Probably.

$$\frac{60}{\text{OUP}} \rightarrow \frac{1}{2} st^2$$

Recommended Reading

BOOKS

Want to brush up on your bug knowledge? Here's a list of books dedicated to creepy-crawlies.

Glaser, Linda. *Not a Buzz to Be Found.* Minneapolis: Millbrook Press, 2012.

Heos, Bridget. *What to Expect When You're Expecting Larvae: A Guide for Insect Parents (and Curious Kids).* Minneapolis: Millbrook Press, 2011.

Markle, Sandra. Insect World series. Minneapolis: Lerner Publications, 2008.

WEBSITES

Find out more about nature and wildlife using the websites below.

BioKids

http://www.biokids.umich.edu/critters/
The University of Michigan's Critter Catalog has

a ton of pictures of different kinds of bugs and information on where they live, how they behave, and their predators.

National Geographic Kids
http://video.nationalgeographic.com/video/kids
/animals-pets-kids/bugs-kids
Go to this fun website to watch clips from National Geographic about all sorts of creepy-crawlies.

U.S. Fish & Wildlife Service
http://www.fws.gov/letsgooutside/kids.html
This website has lots of activities for when you're outside playing and looking for wildlife.

CHECK OUT ALL OF THE

#1 Spider Stampede

Eight-year-olds Josh and Danny discover that their neighbor Miss Potts has a secret formula that can change people into bugs. Soon enough, they find themselves with six extra legs. Can the boys survive in the world as spiders long enough to make it home in time for dinner?

#2 Fly Frenzy

Danny and Josh are avoiding their neighbor because she "accidentally" turned them into bugs. But when their mom's garden is ruined the day before a big competition, the twins turn into bluebottle houseflies to discover the culprits. Will they find who's responsible before it's too late?

#3 Grasshopper Glitch

Danny and Josh are having a normal day at school . . . until they turn into grasshoppers in the middle of class! Can they avoid being eaten during their whirlwind search to find the antidote? And will they be able to change back before getting a week of detention?

 TITLES!

#4 Ant Attack

Danny and Josh are being forced to play with Tarquin, the most annoying boy in the neighborhood. But things get dangerous when the twins accidentally turn into ants and discover that Tarquin kills bugs for fun. . . . Can they find a safe place to hide until they turn human again?

#5 Crane Fly Crash

When Petty Potts leaves town, she puts Danny and Josh in charge of some of her S.W.I.T.C.H. spray. Unfortunately, their sister, Jenny, mistakes it for hair spray and ends up as a crane fly. Now it's up to the twins to keep Jenny from being eaten alive.

#6 Beetle Blast

Danny is forced to go with his brother, Josh, to his nature group, but neither of them thought they would turn into the nature they were studying! Both brothers become beetles just in time to learn about pond dipping . . . from the bug's perspective. Can they avoid getting caught by the other kids?

About the Author

Ali Sparkes grew up in the woods of Hampshire, England. Actually, strictly speaking, she grew up in a house in Hampshire. The woods were great but lacked basic facilities like sofas and a well-stocked fridge. Nevertheless, the woods were where she and her friends spent much of their time, and so Ali grew up with a deep and abiding love of wildlife. If you ever see Ali with a large garden spider on her shoulder, she will most likely be screeching, "AAAARRRGHGETITOFFME!"

Ali lives in Southampton with her husband and sons. She would never kill a creepy-crawly of any kind. They are more scared of her than she is of them. (Creepy-crawlies, not her husband and sons.)

About the Illustrator

Ross Collins's more than eighty picture books and books for young readers have appeared in print around the world. He lives in Scotland and, in his spare time, enjoys leaning backward precariously in his chair.